Books by Alex Cliff
SUPERPOWERS series

SUPER POWERS

THE DEADLY STINK

PUFFIN BOOKS

Published by the Penguin Group
Penguin Books Ltd, 80 Strand, London WC2R 0RL, England
Penguin Group (USA) Inc., 375 Hudson Street, New York, New York 10014, USA
Penguin Group (Canada), 90 Eglinton Avenue East, Suite 700, Toronto, Ontario, Canada M4P 2Y3
(a division of Pearson Penguin Canada Inc.)
Penguin Ireland, 25 St Stephen's Green, Dublin 2, Ireland (a division of Penguin Books Ltd)
Penguin Group (Australia), 250 Camberwell Road, Camberwell, Victoria 3124, Australia
(a division of Pearson Australia Group Pty Ltd)
Penguin Books India Pvt Ltd, 11 Community Centre, Panchsheel Park,
New Delhi – 110 017, India
Penguin Group (NZ), 67 Apollo Drive, Rosedale, North Shore 0632, New Zealand
(a division of Pearson New Zealand Ltd)
Penguin Books (South Africa) (Pty) Ltd, 24 Sturdee Avenue, Rosebank,
Johannesburg 2196, South Africa

Penguin Books Ltd, Registered Offices: 80 Strand, London WC2R 0RL, England

puffinbooks.com

Published 2007
1

Set in Bembo
Typeset by Palimpsest Book Production Limited, Grangemouth, Stirlingshire
Made and printed in England by Clays Ltd, St Ives plc

British Library Cataloguing in Publication Data
A CIP catalogue record for this book is available from the British Library

ISBN: 978-0-141-32135-6

To Alec and Callum Purcell, and to Emma,

for thinking up such a brilliant idea!

CONTENTS

JUST IMAGINE . . .

a full moon shining down on a grey ruined castle. In the village below the castle, the church clock strikes eight. As the final chime rings out a hawk shoots like a deadly arrow down from the night sky. Seconds later there is a high-pitched squeal and the brown-grey bird rises, clutching a rabbit in its claws. Settling on the ruined battlement it grabs a mouthful and then swoops abruptly into the castle's one remaining tower.

There is a thunderclap and suddenly a woman is standing in the doorway of the tower. She is twice as tall as a normal woman and wears a cloak of brown-grey feathers. This is Juno, the evil goddess. Touching her finger to the corner of her mouth she delicately

wipes away a small scrap of fur before turning and speaking into the tower. 'So another day is over, Hercules.' She clicks her fingers. Inside the tower the stones on the far wall begin to crumble, leaving a rectangular hole.

A man looks out of it. His face is lined but noble. 'Yes, and I have another of my superpowers back.' Hercules stares defiantly at the goddess. 'That is two of my powers I have back now, Juno – my speed and my strength.'

'But you need to get all seven powers back if you are to escape from the walls of this tower,' Juno reminds him. 'And you only have five days left, Hercules.'

Hercules lifts his chin. 'The two boys from the village will go on helping me.

They have shown they are resourceful and brave.'

Juno snorts in derision. 'They have shown nothing of the sort. They have succeeded these last two days by mere luck. And soon,' her eyes glint darkly, 'their luck will run out.'

'You underestimate them, Juno,'

Hercules says with quiet confidence. 'I believe they are true heroes.'

'Really?' Juno raises her eyebrows. 'Well, we shall see tomorrow when they have the task of cleaning out the impossibly dirty stables – one thousand years of dung to move before sunset. Do you believe they will manage it?'

'Yes,' Hercules replies loyally, 'I do.'

'Ah.' A slow dangerous smile crosses Juno's face 'But *that* is because you do not know what I have got planned.' She laughs gleefully. 'The task might be *just* a little harder than you think, Hercules.'

Hercules' confidence fades. 'Juno! What are you planning? What –'

'You'll find out.' The goddess clicks her fingers. 'Tomorrow.' The stones instantly re-form over Hercules' face.

Juno walks to the doorway of the tower and looks out towards the village. 'And so will they!'

She claps her hands. A lightning bolt shoots down from the sky. But this time the lightning does not fork down to the ground but curls into a round shape with six legs. The image lights up the sky and then vanishes.

Seconds later, a hawk bursts from the tower and disappears into the night.

CHAPTER ONE

THE CALM BEFORE THE STORM

Max Hayward was sitting on the floor doing his half-term homework. 'How many men does it take to move one thousand, five hundred and eighty-four bricks if each man can carry twelve bricks?' he read out to his best friend, Finlay Yates.

'Who cares?' Finlay replied. He was building a Lego Technic model. His homework was untouched beside him. 'Those men should just stick the bricks in a lorry! It's a dumb question.'

'Yeah,' Max said, giving up and closing his book. 'I guess I can finish it tomorrow.'

'You're mental, doing your homework so early. I'm not going to do mine till Sunday,' Finlay said. He stretched.

'Ouch! My shoulder's really sore.' He pulled back the neck of his T-shirt. On his shoulder blade there was a deep cut.

Max went over to inspect it. Blood oozed from the corners of the wound. 'It looks like a pair of wings,' he said. 'Bet it's going to turn into a scar. Do you think we should tell my mum?'

'Nah. She'll only want to know how I did it,' Finlay replied. 'And we can't tell her the truth.'

Max nodded. He could just imagine his mum's reaction if they told her that Finlay had been stabbed by a fang from a nine-headed river monster. She'd never believe it. It was hard enough to believe it himself and he'd been there!

It was amazing what had happened to their lives in the last two days.

Before then, he and Finlay had just been normal eight-year-old boys living normal lives, but now they had this huge secret that no one knew about. They were spending their days fighting monsters and completing impossible tasks. It had all started when they had found the superhero Hercules trapped inside the walls of the castle tower they used as their den. Max and Finlay had listened in disbelief as Hercules had told them how the evil goddess Juno had defeated him in a mega-battle and then imprisoned him inside the tower walls. The only way that Hercules might escape was if he regained all seven of the superpowers that Juno had stolen from him. She had placed them in the stones around the castle gatehouse entrance opposite his tower.

Max and Finlay were determined to help and so they had struck a deal with Juno. Every day she would set them a task. If they completed it before sunset Hercules would get one of his superpowers back. If they failed then the superpower would vanish. Forever. The cool thing was that each day either Max or Finlay got to take one of Hercules' amazing superpowers out of the stones to help them with the task. The less cool thing was the chance that they might die each day. So far they'd managed to avoid it but they had both been wounded – Max on the first day and Finlay on the second. Max looked at Finlay's injury again and suddenly realized something.

'It's weird your scar looks like a pair of wings,' he pointed out. He looked at the scar on his left hand from two days ago. 'And mine looks like a hammer.'

'Yeah,' Finlay agreed, peering at them.

'They're just like the symbols of the superpowers in the stones, aren't they?'

Max nodded. Every morning Hercules' trapped superpowers shone out of the stones in the gatehouse wall. Each power appeared as a different picture or symbol. The superpower he'd chosen on the first day – strength – had been shown on the wall as a picture of a hammer; the superpower Finlay had chosen that morning – speed – had been shown by a picture of a pair of wings. Now he had a hammer-shaped scar and Finlay had a scar in the shape of a pair of wings. 'Do you think we'll get a scar every day?' he said slowly.

'I don't know.' Finlay thought for a moment and then grinned. 'It would be cool if we did, though, wouldn't it?'

Max nodded but he wasn't completely sure. The wound on his hand still hurt.

At least the task tomorrow doesn't sound too dangerous, he comforted himself. Juno had said she was going to make them clean out some impossibly dirty stables. It sounded gross but not scary in a monster-with-fangs kind of way. He couldn't see any way that poo could give either one of them a scar. 'I'm glad we've only got stables to clean out tomorrow,' he told Finlay. 'Poo's not scary and it can't hurt us.'

'Yeah, it's not as if it's got teeth or anything,' Finlay agreed, still looking at his scar. 'It's just stinky.'

'Imagine poo with teeth!' Max said with a laugh. 'Now that would be cool!'

Finlay grinned. 'They could make a

film about it.' He put on a spooky voice. 'The Revenge of the Killer Poo!'

Max snorted.

'Or how about The Curse of the Were-poo,' Finlay sniggered. 'Or King Poo.'

'Superpoo,' Max added, making a rude noise. 'A poo in shorts.'

They both cracked up. 'Come on.' Max stood up. 'Let's go and see if Dad's finished putting up my new bunk beds yet.'

'Doctor Poo,' Finlay said as they went up the stairs. 'A poo in a TARDIS.'

Sniggering, they went into the bedroom. Max's dad was standing back, looking at the set of bunk beds he'd been building. He had a confused expression on his face.

Finlay stared. 'Um . . . are the beds supposed to be leaning like that, Mr Hayward?'

'Yeah, Dad,' Max said. 'They don't look right.' The whole bed-frame was tilting to one side.

Mr Hayward scratched his head. 'I know. I've got all these bits left over that I shouldn't have. I can't work out where they should go. The plan's impossible to follow.'

Finlay looked at the bits of wood on the floor and then began walking round the bunk beds, frowning thoughtfully. Max went to look at the plan his dad was holding. It was just a load of drawings of pieces of wood and screws. He could see why his dad was looking confused.

'Maybe I should just start again tomorrow,' Mr Hayward sighed. 'You two had better sleep in the spare room tonight.'

'I think you've missed out one of the parts here,' Finlay said, picking up a length of wood and peering underneath the top bunk. 'If you fix this here,' he showed Mr Hayward what he meant, 'it will stop the beds leaning and help support the frame. I'll help you if you want.'

'Goodness!' said Max's dad. 'I think you're right! However did you work that out, Finlay?'

'It was easy,' Finlay shrugged. 'I just looked at the bits you had left and looked at the beds.'

Max wasn't surprised. Finlay was brilliant at making things. He was always messing around with Lego Technic and stuff like that. 'What about this big panel here, then?' he asked, wobbling a long piece of wood. 'I found it behind the door!'

'I forgot about that,' Mr Hayward admitted.

Finlay smiled. 'That must go under the bottom bunk. You'll need metal pins to keep it in place.'

Together they fixed all the missing pieces. Once Mr Hayward had added the ladder and the mattresses, the bunk beds were complete.

'All done!' he said in relief. There was a flash of lightning outside. 'Looks like there's a storm brewing. I'd better pack my tools away in the shed before it starts to rain.'

He carried his tools downstairs and the boys began getting ready for bed.

'I'll set my alarm clock,' Max said. 'We've got to be at the castle early.'

'We'll need all the time we can get to clean those stables,' Finlay agreed.

'We're going to do this task!' declared Max. 'We're going to get another superpower back for Hercules.'

Finlay grinned. 'Yeah! We'll defeat the poo!' He held up his hand and Max met it in a high five.

Through the window behind them neither boy noticed a white lightning fork curling round. For a moment it blazed out in the shape of a giant beetle. A thunderclap crashed and the shape was gone, leaving just a faint creepy shadow in the sky . . .

CHAPTER TWO

THE WRITING ON THE WALL

Max and Finlay woke up early the next day. Grabbing a banana and a packet of crisps each for their breakfast, they set off to the castle. They borrowed two spades from Mr Hayward's shed.

'Lucky your dad still hasn't noticed that the spade we borrowed the other day is missing,' Finlay pointed out.

'Yeah,' Max replied. Two days ago he'd

had Hercules' power of super-strength. While he'd been testing out his new strength he'd managed to bend one of his dad's spades in two.

Finlay spotted an old metal bath at the side of the path. It was turned upside down. He couldn't resist. 'Hi-yah!' he exclaimed, jumping on to the bath and holding the spade he was carrying over his head. He tried to

bend it, but the spade stayed firm.

'Cool, Fin.' Max grinned. 'Those poos will be shaking in fear.'

'It must have been brilliant being super-strong the other day,' Finlay said, jumping down.

Max nodded. 'Wish I could be again. Size-shifting will be a wicked power to have, though,' he said. 'Imagine being the biggest person in the world and being able to crush people to mush!' They had talked long into the night about which superpower Max should choose to help them with the stables. Max had already been super-strong and Finlay had been super-fast. There was accuracy, agility, size-shifting, defence and courage left. After much debate they'd decided that size-shifting sounded the most useful power.

A shiver of excitement ran through Finlay as he thought about it. Any superpower would be great to have. He wished it was his turn again that day!

Max looked at the sun rising above the castle. 'Come on! The sun will be shining on the gatehouse wall. I can get the power now.'

For twenty minutes every morning, just as the sun's rays fell on the gatehouse, the stones in front of Hercules' face crumbled and the powers shone out of the gatehouse wall. The power had to be taken before the twenty minutes were up.

Max and Finlay broke into a run. To get to the tower they had to cross the bridge and clamber through the ruined gatehouse. The gatehouse was more ruined now than it had been a week ago because when he'd been super-strong Max had thrown a boulder in the air and accidentally sent it crashing into the gatehouse roof. And the day before Max and Fin had been sheltering in there when the river monster's heads had attacked the walls as they tried to get to the boys. There were stones lying all over the floor. The boys climbed over them and out into the castle keep.

'Boys.' A voice rang out from the tower. Max and Finlay hurried over. Hercules was looking out from the hole in the wall. 'You have come to complete your next task.'

'We have,' Finlay replied. 'We're totally going to get another superpower back for you today.'

Max nodded. 'Yeah. I thought I'd use size-shifting to help.'

'Size-shifting is a good choice,' Hercules agreed. His voice was much stronger than when the boys had first seen him two days ago; his face looked less grey and the wrinkles seemed less deep. With every power he got back, the superhero seemed to strengthen a little more. 'It will let you grow to the size of Jupiter, the king of the gods – many times the height of a normal man.'

'Will I be able to shrink too?' Max asked. He thought that being tiny would be almost as much fun as being super-tall.

'No,' Hercules replied. 'You will be able to grow taller but not smaller. Superpowers make humans god-like.' He looked at the gatehouse anxiously. 'You had better fetch the power while the symbols are shining.'

Max looked at the five remaining symbols that were traced in burning white fire around the gatehouse archway – an arrow, a leaping stag, a shield, a lion, and a tree with an acorn. As well as the five symbols there was some spiky writing glowing on the gatehouse archway. 'Look, Fin,' he said. 'That writing's not usually there.'

'It's a message from Juno, I think,' said Finlay. He read out the words: '*Puny boys, your task today is to clear the old castle stables of a thousand years of dung. The task will be completed when the stables are empty*. Charming,' he commented.

'But you know the task sounds OK today,' he said to Max.

Max nodded. 'At least she's told us where the stables are.' The day before they'd spent ages trying to find the river monster because Juno had decided not to tell them where it was lurking.

'Wait. What's that?' Finlay said, suddenly noticing a small drawing at the end of the message.

Max looked at the round squiggle with lines coming out of it. 'A plate?'

'Or a spider?' Finlay said, peering at it. 'Maybe those lines are supposed to be legs?'

'It would have to be a beetle, then,' Max pointed out. 'It's only got six legs.'

'Quick, boys. It is time to get the power,' Hercules urged. 'The sun is passing by. The symbols will soon be gone.'

Max took a deep breath. As he looked at the white burning pictures his heart thumped in his chest. He was about to get a superpower for the day! Fixing his eyes on the tree and acorn – the symbol for size-shifting – Max stepped forward and banged his hand on to the picture . . .

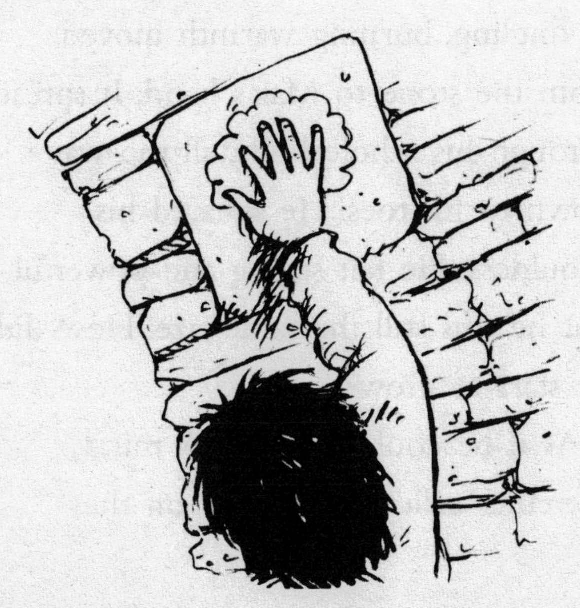

CHAPTER THREE

BIG MAX!

A tingling, burning warmth moved from the stone to Max's hand. It spread through his whole body, all the way down to his toes. He squared his shoulders. He felt strong and powerful, but he was still the same size. How did he start to grow?

As if he could read Max's mind, Hercules called out, 'Draw on the power inside yourself, boy.'

Max shut his eyes. He could feel his heart pumping strongly, his ears seemed to sing. *Grow,* he thought, *I want to grow*. He frowned in concentration. *Grow* . . .

Suddenly he felt himself shooting upwards as if he was in a very fast lift.

'Max!' Finlay gasped.

Max's eyes shot open. They were level with the top window on the tower. 'Wow!' he exclaimed, realizing that he

could see over the castle walls and out across the fields and woods. He looked down. He hadn't just stretched upwards like a piece of spaghetti; his body had grown widthways too. He was a giant!

A pigeon flew at him. With an alarmed squawk, it banked upwards and shot over his head. Its eyes looked astonished as it took in the god-sized Max.

'Wicked!' Finlay exclaimed. His voice sounded faint and far away. 'You're really big, Max!' He laughed. 'Hey, if I call you Big Max it makes you sound like a burger!'

Max grinned. Finlay's head was level with his knees. 'This is so cool!' He strode around the castle keep in six giant strides. 'I can see for miles!' Max stopped by the gatehouse. He could reach the roof. The enormous stones that had fallen looked like pebbles at his feet. Bending over, he picked them up easily and slotted them back into the spaces in the roof. They were still a bit wobbly because he didn't have any cement, but it made Max feel better about the damage they'd caused.

'This is so amazing,' he said, striding over to Hercules and looking down at the superhero. 'How do I get back to normal size?'

'Look inside yourself, boy,' Hercules said softly.

Max concentrated hard. *Be small, be small*, he thought. To his surprise he felt himself whizzing downwards. It was like being a telescope as it was made smaller.

'You were enormous!' Finlay exclaimed. 'What was it like?'

A smile spread across Max's face. 'Brilliant!'

'Lucky your clothes grew with you,' Finlay pointed out.

'Very!' Max grinned at the thought of what would have happened if they hadn't. 'Hey, this is great! We'll be able to clear the stables out easily with me that big. I'll be able to move loads of muck.'

'Yeah,' Finlay said. 'Let's go and get started!'

'Good luck!' Hercules called as the stones in the wall began to close back over his face.

Grabbing their spades the boys hurried out of the gatehouse and down the hill. Near the bottom of the hill the footpath forked. They took the right turn that led to the woods. The old castle stables stood just where the woods began, near a small stream.

'This task's going to be easy,' Max said as they approached the stables. They had been built of stone, but over the years many of the stones had fallen away and the walls had been patched up with planks of wood. A few grey slates had fallen off the inner wooden beams, leaving holes exposed to the sky. As the boys approached, a horrid stink wafted towards them.

'Poo!' Max pulled a face.

Finlay covered his mouth and nose with his hands. 'You said it!' Their footsteps slowed as they approached the stables. A dark-brown sludge was oozing out from under the wooden door.

As they got closer the smell grew stronger. It seemed to thicken the air.

'Do we really have to go in there?' Finlay said, holding his nose and trying to breathe through his mouth to block out the worst of the smell.

''Fraid we do,' Max gulped. He put his hand on the door and pulled. It creaked on its hinges. As it swung open a wave of warm smelly air hit them in the face. It stank of rotten eggs and farmyards. Max and Finlay both coughed and spluttered.

'Gross!' Finlay exclaimed.

Holding his hand firmly over his mouth Max peered inside the stables. Muck reached halfway up the walls; near the top were brown balls of horse poo and then it seemed to go down in layers getting darker and darker. The muck at the bottom of the pile was so dark it was almost black.

'This is going to be horrible,' Finlay groaned.

'At least it's better than fighting a monster. We should be able to get the muck out of here by sunset and then Hercules can have his power back.' Max drew a deep breath to give himself courage but then instantly regretted it. The stench hit the back of his throat and filled his lungs. 'Yeugh!'

'Max,' Finlay said slowly. 'Look at the muck!'

Max stared. The surface of the muck seemed to be trembling. It quivered, the brown balls of poo moving slightly from side to side. 'What . . . what's happening?'

'I don't know.' Finlay took a step back. 'But I don't like it, Max!'

'It's like there's something *in* the muck,' Max said. 'Something underneath the top layer like . . . Argh!' Suddenly thousands of black, shiny, muck-coated beetles erupted from out of the dung. They shot upwards, their mucky wings whirring, their eyes glowing like red pinpricks in the dim light. Bits of crusty poo flew everywhere and the air was filled with a horrible buzzing.

'Beetles!' Finlay yelled as the beetles flew above the muck. 'Millions of them!'

The beetles swivelled towards the boys. There was a horrible pause where every beetle seemed to stare at Max and Finlay. Then suddenly all the beetles moved as one and zoomed like tiny black torpedoes straight at the two boys!

CHAPTER FOUR

BEATING THE BEETLES!

'Get off!' Max yelled as the beetles dive-bombed him and Finlay. The beetles' wings whirred and their pincers scratched at the boys' faces and arms. Max shut his eyes as a group of beetles zoomed for his eyeballs.

'Let's get out of here!' Finlay gasped.

Dropping their spades, he and Max ran out of the door. To their relief the beetles didn't come outside. They flew back to the pile of muck and settled down on the top of the balls of poo.

'Look at them all!' Max exclaimed.

Finlay shuddered as he looked at the buzzing mass. 'Looks like you were right about Juno's picture – it *was* a beetle.'

'I guess it's not that bad,' Max said. 'I mean, I know there's a lot of them but they're just tiny beetles, not monsters.

We can squash them and then get started on clearing out the stables. If I grow big, then I'll be able to squash loads of them at once.'

Finlay nodded. 'Good idea.'

They went back inside the stables. Immediately the beetles flew at them, their hard bodies battering into the boys' faces and hair.

'Get off!' Fin exclaimed, waving his hands in front of his face and trying to see through the whirring mass of furious beetles.

Max shut his eyes and thought hard. *Grow. I want to grow.* He felt the strange sensation of shooting up in a lift again and opened his eyes just as his head thwacked into the roof of the stables.

'Ow!' he exclaimed.

'Stop growing!' Finlay shouted frantically as Max squashed harder and harder against the roof. The stables' timber beams began to creak alarmingly.

Max shut his eyes. *Stop growing*, he thought. To his relief he stopped getting any bigger but he still had to stoop to fit inside. His arms and legs pushed against the stable walls. He could hardly move, he was squashed in so tight. 'I'll have to shrink a bit,' he called down, trying not to swallow a cloudful of beetles. 'I can't do anything when I'm so big.'

Shutting his eyes, he managed to shrink himself so that when he was standing up straight his head was no longer bumping into the roof. It was still difficult to move around the stables, though, so he shrank a bit more until he was about twice the size of a normal man. 'That's better!' he exclaimed. 'Let's get these beetles!'

Finlay grabbed a spade and swiped at them. *Thwack!* It knocked a load to the floor. Finlay jumped on them. *Crunch!* The beetles' shells cracked under his feet like popcorn popping in a pan. 'Die, beetles!' he exclaimed.

'Yeah, die, you beetle scum!' Max cried, stamping his newly huge feet up and down and swiping in the air with his big hands.

But to their surprise, although the beetles crunched and cracked, they didn't die. As soon as the boys stopped stamping on them the beetles straightened their legs, got up, shook themselves and took off into the air again, buzzing even more angrily.

'What's going on?' Finlay exclaimed, looking up at Max. 'We don't even seem to be hurting them.'

'They must be evil supernatural beetles!' Max said. 'Beetles that can't be killed.'

'What are we going to do?' Finlay said.

'I guess we just have to try and ignore them,' replied Max. He yelled as a beetle zoomed into his ear and shook his head frantically. The beetle buzzed out. 'We might not be able to kill them, but they're only small and they can't stop us clearing out the muck.'

'We could cover our mouths with

our jumpers, so we don't swallow any of them,' Finlay said.

'Good idea!' Max ducked as a gang of beetles dive-bombed his head from the rafters.

The boys pulled off their jumpers and tied them round their faces, covering their mouths.

'Now to clear the muck!' Max said in a muffled voice. 'Where's the other spade?'

Fin picked it up and held it out. The

same thought hit both Max and Finlay at the same time.

'Oh no,' Finlay groaned. 'Even though you're big, the spade isn't. You're not going to be able to move the muck any faster with it.'

Max hit his forehead. 'Of course. I thought if I was big then I could move the muck easily, but I'd need a giant-sized spade to do that.'

'Or . . .' Finlay looked at Max's big hands. 'You could just use your hands.'

Max looked at the pile of steaming dung. 'Oh, gross!' he muttered. But he knew Finlay was right. They needed to get the stables cleared before sunset. Time was running out and using his hands was going to be the best way of moving the muck.

Gritting his teeth, he plunged his hands into the dung. It oozed warm and soft between his fingers. The beetles crawled over his hands, their tiny pincers biting at his skin. Trying not to breathe in the revolting stench Max picked up a large handful and carried it to the doorway, his arms outstretched. 'This is *so* not fun!' Pulling a face, he dumped the stinky poo and then headed back into the stables and picked up another armful. 'And it's going to take ages!'

'We're going to have to be as quick as we can,' Fin said. He got a spade to start helping, but as they headed back to the stables a second time they were stopped in their tracks by the sight of all the beetles scurrying out of the doorway towards the pile of dung.

'What are they doing?' Finlay asked in amazement.

The boys watched as the beetles picked up every single piece of muck with their front legs and began to hurry back to the stables with it.

'Stop it!' Finlay exclaimed, jumping in front of them and trying to block their way. 'You can't take it back in!' But the beetles ignored him, scuttling past his feet and carrying their muck back into the stables.

'I guess they live in it,' Max said. 'And they want it back in the stables.'

'Well, they can live in it out here,' Finlay said. 'Come on! We're going to have to be extra quick if we've got to beat them!'

But as fast as the boys got rid of the

muck the beetles carried it back again. Although they were only small, there were thousands of them and they worked tirelessly.

'This is useless!' Finlay said when, after an hour of hard work, the boys looked at the pile of muck they had managed to remove. It was tiny. 'We're never going to clear the stables!'

'If we don't get it done by sunset Hercules will lose his size-shifting ability forever,' said Max, feeling very worried. 'He can't break free from the tower without all seven of his superpowers.'

'And what will Juno do to us if we fail in the task?' added Finlay.

Max looked round. 'We've got to do something,' he said urgently. 'We've got to find some way of getting the muck out of the stables more quickly.'

Finlay looked at the scurrying, busy beetles. 'Or at least think of a way of stopping the beetles carting it all back in straight away.'

'But how can we do that?' Max said.

A smile spread across Finlay's face. 'You know, I think I've got an idea!'

CHAPTER FIVE

FINLAY'S IDEA

Max stared at Finlay. 'You've thought of something we can do to stop the beetles?'

Finlay nodded. 'What we need to do is to trap them in something, so they won't be able to fly at us and carry the poo back into the stables.'

'It'll need to be something pretty big to trap them all in,' Max pointed out.

'I've thought of that,' replied Finlay. 'We could use the old bath back down the path. You could grow tall and carry it here. We can bring out some muck and wait till all the beetles come to get it and then drop it on them!'

'Cool!' Max said. Getting rid of the horrible buzzing beetles sounded like a great plan and maybe then they'd be able to get a move on with shifting the muck. 'Let's go and get the bath.' He shut his eyes and grew as tall as he could.

They set off down the path, with Finlay running to keep up with Max. 'Hope we don't bump into anyone,' he panted.

'Me too,' Max said. 'Imagine what they'd say if they saw me like this!'

'Imagine what they'd *smell*,' added

Finlay, looking down at his crusty clothes.

Luckily there was no one on the footpath. The boys reached the rusty old bath. It was beside a crumbling brick well that was covered over by a wooden lid.

Max looked at the bath. 'This is perfect!' he said, bending down and hoicking it easily on to his broad shoulders. 'Now all we need to do is get the beetles together.'

That was easy. As soon as they got

back to the stables Max shrank a bit and then went inside and fetched a huge armful of muck. The beetles buzzed around him. Fighting his way through them, he carried the muck to the door and chucked it outside. Half the beetles rushed out to rescue it. Max threw another armful as fast as he could and then another. Soon all the beetles were racing out of the stables to bring the muck back.

Grabbing a spade, Finlay shoved the muck into a bath-sized mound. The beetles swarmed towards it. As they reached it Max ran to the bath and picked it up.

'Now!' Finlay shouted.

'Gotcha!' Max exclaimed, throwing the bath over the beetles and the muck.

The beetles went wild. Max and Finlay could hear them whirring round inside the bath, their wings beating furiously at the rusty metal, but they couldn't escape.

'Yes!' Finlay said. He lifted his hand in a high five and then, looking at Max's muck-stained arms, quickly changed his mind. 'We've got them!'

Max breathed a sigh of relief. 'Now we can move the muck in peace.'

'I'm starving,' Finlay said.

'We haven't got time to stop for lunch,' Max told him. 'We're running out of time!'

They hurried back into the stables. A few remaining beetles buzzed furiously at them, but the boys took no notice. Finlay began shovelling the muck out

and Max began to carry great armfuls again. They worked as fast as they could and the pile outside began to grow, but it was very tiring work. Soon they were both sweating.

'My arms are aching,' Finlay complained.

'Mine too,' Max replied as he ducked into the stables after dumping another armful of dung. 'But at least we're getting rid of the muck. Look, we seem to be down to a different layer.' He pointed to the mountain of dung. They had cleared the top light-brown layer of round poos and had reached a point where the muck was darker and squishier.

'It's much easier now we've got rid of the beetles,' Finlay said.

'Yeah,' Max agreed. 'We might just manage to get it all out by sunset and –' He broke off as a movement in the muck caught his eye. The surface of the next layer of muck was quivering. It started to tremble and move. 'Look!' he exclaimed.

The two boys stared at the muck.

Finlay started shaking his head. 'This doesn't look good . . .'

Suddenly hundreds more beetles exploded out of the muck. But they were all ten times the size of the first beetles. They were as big as dinner plates! Their pincers clicked open and closed like sharp scissors as they flew straight at Max and Finlay.

'Arrgh!' Max and Finlay yelled together.

'Incoming!' warned Max, grabbing Finlay and pulling him down as a particularly large beetle shot towards Finlay's head.

'Outgoing!' Fin shouted, heading swiftly for the door. One of the beetles landed on his head and got tangled in his hair. He yelled and yanked it out.

He and Max shot out into the fresh air. The beetles filled the doorway like a buzzing black curtain, their evil eyes glowing, their pincers snapping.

'They're huge!' Max panted, turning round and staring at the beetles. 'We can't clear the muck out with them in there!'

'But we must,' said Fin.

'How?' Max exclaimed.

'We'll just have to trap these ones too!' Finlay replied. He thought for a moment,

his mind working fast. 'I know. How about the well? It's got a lid. You could take a load of muck up there and dump it inside. If the beetles follow we can stick the lid on and trap them like that.'

Max swallowed. He didn't fancy all those giant beetles flying after him as he ran up the hill. But what choice did they have? 'OK. But how am I going to get into the stables to get the muck in the first place?'

Fin picked up his spade and put on a voice like a cop in a TV movie. 'Don't worry,' he said. 'I'll cover you. But first we need to take the lid off the well.'

Max nodded and strode up the path to remove the lid from the well. When he came back Finlay was waiting by the stable door. The beetles were flying round inside, cannoning off the walls with thumps and thuds.

The boys looked at each other. 'You ready?' Finlay asked.

Max took a deep breath and nodded. 'It's now or never! One, two . . .'

'*Three!*' they both yelled as they ran into the stables, side by side. Finlay swiped the spade around. The big beetles thwacked into it. Each one that collided with his spade was sent whizzing across the stables, legs whirring, red eyes furious.

Max grabbed the biggest armful of muck he could. His eyes streamed as the stink hit him in the face. Turning, he ran out. The beetles shot after him. Max raced up the hill with the beetles chasing him, their pincers snapping.

Max could hear the buzzing of their wings. It got louder and louder as the beetles began to catch up. His heart pounded. They were bearing down on him. They were going to get him! He could see the well at the top of the track. Just a few more strides. Was he going to make it?

CHAPTER SIX

THE MUCK MOVES AGAIN . . .

Max's foot caught in the grass. He stumbled forward. The muck sailed out of his arms and landed mostly in the well. Lying flat on his face Max felt the beetles stream past him and fly down the well after it. Panting hard, he scrambled to his feet, kicked the rest of the dung after them, grabbed the wooden lid and slammed it down.

He'd got them!

He turned and saw Finlay running up the path towards him. 'You did it!'

Max nodded in relief. 'Let's get back to the stables.'

'I can't believe there were more beetles,' Finlay said as they went inside and began shifting the muck again.

'And bigger ones,' Max replied. 'They were horrid.'

They dug and carried as fast as they could. The day was passing and the stables were still half full of muck.

'I wonder why the last lot of beetles were so much bigger than the first ones,' Finlay panted as they finally reached another layer of dung, even smellier and blacker than the last.

Max looked at the black dung and a

horrid thought struck him. 'You don't think there's new beetles in every layer, do you?'

Finlay looked at him and then at the new layer of muck. 'What, you mean for each layer of muck there's another layer of beetles?'

Max nodded. 'Maybe the deeper down you get, the older the beetles get

– and the bigger they get. They don't seem to die. So, maybe they just keep growing and growing.'

'No!' Finlay said, shaking his head. 'Don't say that!'

'Fin!' Max said, grabbing his arm. 'Look!'

The muck was starting to move. Only this time it didn't quiver – it rippled and shook as if there were some great beast underneath it.

'Quick! Run!' Finlay yelled, but it was too late. Twenty beetles exploded out of the poo, their wings making as much noise as a helicopter's propellers. They were enormous! Each one was as tall as Finlay, with giant snapping pincers and huge red eyes the size of tennis balls.

They flew down and landed in the

doorway. Rising up on their back legs they advanced menacingly on the boys, their pincers opening and shutting like sharp garden shears.

'What are we going to do?' Max gasped, shrinking back against the mountain of muck.

'Panic!' Finlay yelled.

The beetles advanced, hissing. Although they were massive for beetles, Max was still very big. *I should do something*, he thought. But what? The army of beetles looked like something out of a horror film.

'I'll try getting to the door!' Max stepped forward bravely. Almost immediately, the closest beetle lunged forward to meet him. Its pincers snapped shut around his leg.

Max yelled in pain as the pincers bit through his jeans and into his skin. Finlay raced forward with his shovel and banged it down on the beetle's head. It staggered backwards and sank down on to all six legs.

'My leg!' Max said, looking at his jeans. They were ripped where the

pincers had grabbed hold and blood was trickling down his leg. Max knew he would probably have a tree-shaped scar there now – the symbol for size-shifting. He hoped his mum wouldn't see it but he didn't have time to think about that now. 'We've got to get out of here!' he exclaimed as the beetles began to advance again, their eyes on the boys' necks.

'But there's no way to the door,' Finlay gasped as the beetles came closer.

An idea burst into Max's brain. 'Who says we've got to use the door!' Shutting his eyes he thought, *Grow, I've got to grow*. He began to shoot upwards.

'What are you doing, Max?' Finlay shouted 'You'll hit your head!'

Clunk!

'Ow,' Max muttered, but he kept his eyes shut and kept on thinking. *Grow. Grow . . .*

His head and shoulders were pressing against the roof. The timbers were creaking. He could feel slates start to fall outside. He pushed as hard as he could and with a final groan the roof gave way. As the slates crashed to the ground outside Max's head and shoulders shot out through the roof. He grew another metre and then stopped. He was tall enough to get out.

'Max!'

Max looked down. The beetles had surrounded Finlay. They were edging closer. They stopped and buzzed. They looked ready to attack . . .

Max bent down and grabbed Finlay

under the shoulders. He yanked him upwards just as all twenty beetles flew at the spot where Finlay had been. Not expecting him to suddenly vanish upwards they crashed into each other.

Max took advantage of their confusion to clamber out of the stables, shrinking as he did so in case the roof collapsed underneath him. Then he and Finlay scrambled down to the ground together, pale-faced and trembling.

'And we thought this task wouldn't be dangerous like the others,' Finlay said shakily. 'It's the nastiest one yet!'

'I know.' Max gulped. 'How are we going to clean the muck out of the stables now?'

'I don't know,' Finlay said. 'Thanks for rescuing me. I didn't think I was going to get out – well, not alive anyway,' he said with a shiver. 'It was a wicked idea to think of getting out through the roof.'

Max was pleased. 'I could see the

beetles were never going to let us get to the door, but then I realized we didn't *have* to use the door. It was just a case of thinking differently about the problem.'

'Of course!' Finlay gasped, jumping to his feet. 'That's it, Max! That's how we solve this task!'

'What are you on about?' Max said in astonishment.

'Think differently!' Finlay exclaimed. 'We don't have to move the muck. We don't even need to touch it. We can move the *stables* instead!'

CHAPTER SEVEN

A GIANT PUZZLE

Max stared at Finlay. 'We move the stables?' he echoed.

'Yeah!' Finlay was almost jumping up and down in excitement. 'Remember that message. Juno said that the task would be completed when the stables were empty. But she didn't say the stables had to still be in the same place.'

'That's a great idea!' Max breathed.

'It's so simple,' said Finlay. 'The stables are really old – you should be able to pull them apart easily. Then we just put them back together a bit further away.' Finlay's eyes shone. This was one of the best ideas he'd ever had. 'The beetles will stay with the muck. Only the stables will move. And that way the stables will be clear of dung by sunset!'

'But it's a bit of a cheat,' Max said. 'Do you think it'll count if we do it this way?'

'We don't have any choice.' Finlay looked at his watch. 'It's getting late and if we try and move the muck we're going to have to face those beetles.'

'OK, let's move the stables instead,' Max said quickly. There was no way he wanted to go back inside the stables with those killer mutant beetles.

'Go on then!' Finlay said. 'Grow!'

Max grew as tall as he could and strode to the stables. The corners of the stables were still made of stone, but most of the sides were made of planks of wood nailed together.

'Where do I start?' he said to Finlay.

'Easy,' Finlay declared. 'We'll mark out the rough shape of the old stables on the ground where we want our new stables to go. That way we'll know where to place the cornerstones – the first bits of any new building.'

Max understood. 'A bit like the way my dad did the bunk beds.'

'That's right.' Finlay nodded. 'Only the stables will be much less wonky!'

Max grinned. 'That's not hard!'

They chose a place just a few metres to the left of where the stables stood now, and marked a basic plan of the building with sticks and stones.

'You need to start by taking down the roof and working your way down to the ground,' Finlay told Max. 'Otherwise the roof will fall in and we'll have to fight our way past the beetles to pull the slates out from the muck. Come on!' He found a large stone and scrambled up on top of the stable roof. Once up there he started to knock out the old wooden pegs that held the supports in place, so Max could pull everything apart. With his giant's arm span, Max was able to lift almost half the roof in one go, carrying it carefully like a tray of drinks.

Under Finlay's direction Max started prising away the wooden boards and breaking up the stone of the stable walls. Luckily the cement holding them together was very old and the pieces of wall came apart easily. To Max's relief the beetles ignored him while he did it. They were far more interested in guarding the big pile of muck. They crouched on the steaming pile of dung, their red eyes glaring as they watched him taking the stables apart.

'We've done it!' Max exclaimed in relief as he carried over the last chunk of stone to the pile he had made by the stream. But then an awful thought hit him. How were they going to stick all the bits back together?

He looked round. Finlay was crouching by the stream. 'Finlay, how do we put the walls back together without any cement?' Max asked anxiously.

Finlay grinned. 'Aha! Now, just tell me I'm a genius!' He stood up with a handful of brown sticky sludge in his hands.

'We're going to stick it together with poo!' Max exclaimed in astonishment. 'Yuck!'

'No!' Finlay grinned. 'This isn't poo. It's mud, pebbles and water all mixed together. I reckon it will work as a kind of cement. At least well enough to hold everything together for a while. The stables only need to stay up long enough to show Juno they're empty.'

'That's brilliant!' Max cried, striding over to the pieces of wall. 'Let's get putting everything back together then.' He stopped. All the stone segments looked the same to him. Where should he start? 'Er . . . do you know where all the bits go?'

'Course.' Finlay hurriedly ran over. 'Look, I'll pick out the bits and you can put them where I tell you, but we'd better get a move on.' He glanced at the sky where the sun was starting to set.

They began to rebuild the stables as fast as they could. The beetles watched them from the smelly dung pile with suspiciously glinting eyes but left them alone. The walls looked very fragile, so Finlay propped them up with heavy branches, wedged into the ground at an angle.

At last they had four walls standing. The sun was just reaching the horizon.

'We've got to get the roof on now,' Finlay panted. 'We'd better put it together on the ground, then you can stick it on the top.'

Flexing his muscles Max pushed one half of the roof against the other while Finlay started knocking in the wooden pegs. 'When I put the roof in place we'll have finished – and the stables will be empty of muck. Do you think that means we'll have completed the task?' Max asked.

Finlay crossed his fingers. 'Well, we haven't got time to try anything else.' He looked at the setting sun. Only half of it was visible now. 'Come on, Max! Quick!'

Max tried lifting the roof. It was very tricky to move as one big bit and he was worried that if he put it down too hard on the rickety walls they would collapse and then all their hard work would be for nothing. He had an idea and, picking up the roof with difficulty, he placed it on its end, just outside the stables.

'What are you doing?' Finlay demanded.

'It's too risky putting the roof on like that.' Max shrank himself down to normal size and went inside their new stables. 'I'm going to do it from inside.'

'You're wasting time!' Finlay exclaimed impatiently. 'Just pick it up and plonk it on top.'

'No,' Max insisted. 'If the walls collapse we'll have messed everything up.'

Finlay glanced at the sun. It had almost disappeared. Part of him wanted to just get the roof on as quickly as possible, but Max was right. They couldn't risk the stables falling apart. 'OK,' he said anxiously. 'You lift it and I'll give you directions.'

Grow, Max told himself, and felt himself swelling in size. Soon he was tall enough to reach over the walls and pick up the roof. He lifted it high above his head, holding it like a very large hat over the stables. 'That's a bit easier,' he gasped. 'I should be able to put it in place more gently now.'

As Max lowered the roof slowly into

position Finlay hastily called out directions. 'Back a bit,' he shouted. 'To your left . . . no! No, Max, you've come too far forward . . .'

Every muscle straining, sweat seeping from every pore, Max staggered about inside the stables with the roof. By now it felt heavy as lead, and his tired arms

buzzed with pins and needles. 'Fin, I . . . can't . . . I can't hold it much longer,' he gasped.

'OK, looking good,' said Finlay. 'Gently, gently, hold it steady . . . *now*!'

With a last grunt of effort Max set the roof down lightly on the top of the walls. He held his breath, half-expecting the whole lot to come crashing down around his head.

But to his amazement and relief the stables stayed standing!

'Yes!' he cried. *Go small*, he thought to himself. Shrinking back down to his normal size, he rushed out through the door and punched the air. A fraction of the sun still showed above the horizon. 'How cool is that? We rebuilt the stables! We really did it!'

But Finlay was looking very worried. 'Nothing's happened, Max.'

Max's heart sank as he realized Fin was right. Surely there should have been a thunderclap or a flash of lightning to show they'd completed the task? His heart sank and he looked round. The pile of muck was still there, the beetles guarding it watchfully. They'd failed!

'It's all been a waste of time,' he said, looking at the last tiny bit of the sun as it sank into the horizon. 'We haven't done the task after all!'

CHAPTER EIGHT

JUNO

'I was sure this plan would work,' Finlay said. 'We've done what was asked of us – we've emptied the stables of all the muck. Unless . . . yes! I bet that's it!' His eyes lit up and he darted in through the stable door.

'What are you doing?' Max demanded.

'Thought so!' Finlay shouted

triumphantly from inside the stables. He appeared in the stable doorway with a handful of brown pellets in his hand. 'Rabbit poo! I guess that must count as muck too!' He threw it away and stepped out of the stables. The second his feet crossed the threshold there was a thunderclap and as the last curve of the sun finally set the mountain of poo and beetles vanished in a flash of lightning and the stables returned to their rightful place, just as before.

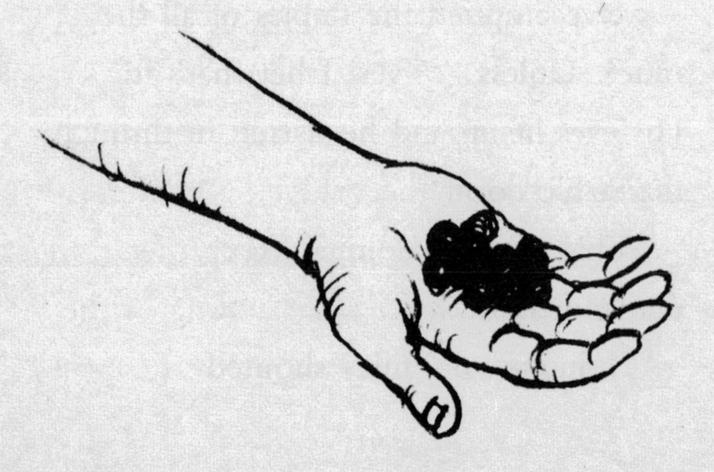

'We did do it!' Max yelled in delight. 'We *were* in time! And now we've got another power back for Hercules!'

He and Finlay exchanged excited high fives.

Finlay grabbed an imaginary microphone and posed like a rock star. 'Goodbye, poo, there was nothing you could do!'

Max grinned. Triumph and relief were racing through him. They'd completed the task! 'Let's see what Juno has got to say for herself now! Come on. Let's get to the castle.'

They ran up the footpath towards the castle and over the bridge. As they scrambled into the inner keep they stopped dead. Juno was standing in the middle and she was looking very angry.

'You cheated!' Her hand shot out towards them. Finlay and Max gasped as they suddenly found themselves frozen in mid-stride.

'We didn't!' Max exclaimed, very relieved to find that although his body wouldn't move he could still speak.

'You didn't clear the dung!' Juno's black eyes flashed and she strode towards them, her cloak of feathers blowing out behind her. 'You moved the stables instead!'

'You didn't say we couldn't,' Finlay protested. 'We completed the task!'

'Yeah,' Max put in. 'You just said we had to empty the stables. You didn't say the stables had to stay in the same place.'

Finlay shivered under the iciness of Juno's gaze.

'Very well!' she snapped. 'Seeing as you completed the task I have no choice but to keep my part of the bargain.' She clicked her fingers.

Max felt a wave of warmth swirl round in his chest. Suddenly it rushed out of him in a stream of golden light, leaving him feeling weak. The light flashed across the grass towards the tower. As it hit the bricks it disappeared and the stones around Hercules' face began to crumble.

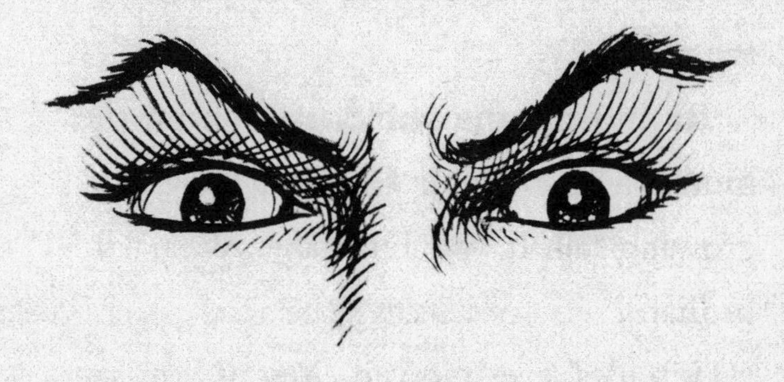

'You did it!' the superhero exclaimed as he became visible. 'I have my power back!' His eyes swept over the two boys and he saw that they were frozen. 'Release them, Juno!' he said angrily. 'They must have completed the task for my superpower to return to me! You cannot hold them like that.'

Looking furious, Juno clapped her hands. The boys were released from her spell. They collapsed to the floor.

'How did you do it?' Hercules demanded of them. 'How did you clear the stables?'

'By moving the stables away from the muck,' Max replied. 'I moved it by growing tall. It was Fin's idea. Wasn't it brilliant?'

Hercules' eyes glowed. 'Yes, as you say,

it was brilliant.' For the first time the boys caught the hint of a smile on his face. 'Well done. That was a very clever solution – you thought like true heroes.'

'You'd better hope that cleverness helps you tomorrow!' Juno snapped.

The boys swung round. The goddess stalked towards them, her eyes hard.

'What have we got to do then?' Finlay asked.

'Before the sun sets you must capture the Giant Boar of Erymanthia,' Juno replied. 'We will see then if you are as heroic as Hercules appears to believe. Real heroes save other people from danger. And so, tomorrow, you must be real heroes – or other people will die.' She clapped her hands angrily.

There was a flash of lightning. When

the boys blinked their eyes open they were alone in the tower. The stones had re-formed over Hercules' face and Juno had vanished.

Max pressed his hand against the wall where Hercules' face had been. 'We'll complete her stupid task,' he muttered. 'We won't let you down. No way.'

'What did she mean about real people dying?' Finlay said.

'Dunno,' Max replied nervously.

'I don't like the sound of a giant boar,' Finlay said.

'I know,' said Max. 'Sounds scary to me.'

'Least the poos didn't have teeth,' Finlay said. He walked into the keep. 'Now that really *would* have been scary.'

Their eyes met and they grinned.

'This boar will have teeth – and tusks, I reckon,' said Max. He looked at Finlay. 'But we'll capture him. We can do anything together!'

Finlay nodded. 'Yes,' he declared. 'We can!'

High overhead the hawk screamed out an angry cry.

ABOUT THE AUTHOR

ALEX CLIFF LIVES IN A VILLAGE IN LEICESTERSHIRE, NEXT DOOR TO FIN AND JUST DOWN THE ROAD FROM MAX, BUT UNFORTUNATELY THERE IS NO CASTLE ON THE OUTSKIRTS OF THE VILLAGE.

ALEX'S HOME IS FILLED WITH TWO CHILDREN AND TWO LARGE AND VERY SLOBBERY PET MONSTERS.

Did you know?

Hercules lived in Ancient Greece. He was the son of a woman named Alcmene and the god Zeus. When Hercules was a baby he could fight snakes with his bare hands! The labours he had to complete were originally set for him by his cousin Eurystheus, King of Mycenae.

The Augean Stables

When Hercules faced this challenge, he had to clean the stables of the largest animal herd in all Greece! He had to divert the course of two rivers so that they flowed through the stables. He completed the task in a single day and, in return, won a tenth of the herd.